MYSTERY ON
CEMETERY HILL

MYSTERY ON CEMETERY HILL

PATRICIA ZEIBER

 iUniverse®

MYSTERY ON CEMETERY HILL

iUniverse books may be ordered through booksellers or by contacting:

iUniverse
1663 Liberty Drive
Bloomington, IN 47403
www.iuniverse.com
844-349-9409

ISBN: 978-1-6632-2708-9 (sc)
ISBN: 978-1-6632-2707-2 (e)

Library of Congress Control Number: 2021921092

Print information available on the last page.

iUniverse rev. date: 10/23/2021

GETTING ACQUAINTED

This is a story about a girl named Olivia Hudskin, who goes on an adventure through life and ends up in a little town called Cemetery Hill. Olivia was eleven years old and lived in Seattle, Washington where she resided with her parents. Her mother Carol was a nurse at the local hospital, her father Harry was a police officer, and her older brother Mark was away at college.

One warm Saturday afternoon Olivia was out riding her bike when she saw a family moving into the house next door. She stopped to see if they had any children then she saw two girls, one that looked about her age and a younger one sitting on the stoop playing with a baby doll. Olivia and the older girl exchanged a smile and a wave then they both stared for a moment and went their separate ways. When Olivia got home she put her bike away, washed her hands, and set the table for her mother. While Olivia and her family had dinner Olivia told her parents she saw a family moving into the house next door. Her mother got up and looked out the curtains and said, "Someone finally bought the Shelby house! I miss Jackie and John, they were nice neighbors. I guess after they get settled in I will bake a cake and we will go over to introduce ourselves and get acquainted".

Then Olivia said, "They have two girls, and one is around my age with red hair, green eyes, and freckles, I hope she will be in my class."

After dinner Olivia helped her mother with the dishes like she always did. Then she watched some television with her father for a while, then she took a shower and went to bed.

Monday morning in class her teacher Mrs. Quigley introduced the new girl.

"Boys and girls, this is our new student, her name is Sarah Johnson. Let's all give her a nice warm welcome and say hello."

All the children said, "Hello Sarah!"

Olivia thought, is she the girl next door?

The girls had lunch together and talked a lot as they got acquainted. They laughed and giggled while they ate their lunch. After school when their homework was done they went out riding their bikes. Soon they became best friends. The following Sunday morning Olivia and her parents were at church and they saw the new neighbors, so after church they shook hands and introduced themselves.

The one woman said to the other, "Hello! My name is Helen Johnson." The other woman replied, "Nice to meet you. I'm Carol Hudskin." Helen said, "This is my husband Mitch and our two daughters, Sarah and Piper."

Olivia's mother Carol said, "It's so nice to meet you. This is my husband Harry, and our daughter Olivia, we also have an older Son Mark, he's away at College."

Helen asked, "What is he studying?"

Carol said, "Arts and film. So Olivia tells me Sarah is in her class and they are already best friends." As the girls giggled and whispered.

Helen said, "Yes I heard, Why don't you and your family stop by later we can get acquainted and the girls can play together."

Carol said, "Sounds good, thanks for the invite, I guess we will see you all later."

That afternoon Carol baked a cake and after dinner they went over to the Johnsons. Helen invited them in and offered them some coffee to have with the cake Carol had brought over.

Carol asked Helen, "Have you and Mitch found a job in the area yet?"

Helen said, "Yes I got a job working at the girl's school in the office, I'm the new secretary and my husband Mitch is a lawyer at the local law firm."

Carol said, "I am a nurse at the hospital and my husband Harry here is a police officer."

Later they had some cocktails and long conversations when Carol realized the time and said, "Look at the time, we'd better be going. It's getting late and the girls have school tomorrow and we all must work in the morning. It's been a pleasure getting to know you and Mitch. Thanks for having us."

Helen said, "I'm so glad you came over and thanks for the cake, we have to do this again sometime."

Carol says, "Looking forward to it."

As the years went by the girls turned fourteen and by now they were inseparable.

They both tried out for cheerleading, and made the team. They played on the girl's volleyball team and got to cheer at all the school basketball and football games and at the school rallies.

They've even gone to summer camps together and had boyfriends.

One day at school the girls had cheerleading practice and since Helen worked in the office, she said she would stay late and drive the girls home when they were done. Their parents have become pretty good friends. Now that the girls are old enough to watch Piper, Sarah's little sister who was nine years old, their parents would go out together for dinners and some drinks occasionally, and Olivia would stay at Sarah's house to help watch Piper.

One night while they were babysitting, they decided after they put Piper to bed they were bored, so Sarah suggested they text their boyfriends and sneak them in for some fun. So Olivia's boyfriend Jeffrey and Sarah's boyfriend Steve came over and kept them entertained with dancing, playing video games, and just hanging out while making sure Piper stayed asleep. They didn't realize what time it was until they heard Sarah's parents pull up in the driveway. So the boys had to hurry up and run out the back door while Sarah and Olivia quickly tidied up the house! When Sarah's parents came into the house the girls were sitting on the couch laughing, Helen asked the girls, "What's so funny?"

They said, "Nothing."

Then Helen said, "Did you girls have a good time?"

And Sarah and Olivia both said, "yes."

Helen said, "Olivia, your mother asked me to send you home dear."

Olivia says "Ok, thank you, Mrs. Johnson, good night."

Sarah's father Mitch watched as Olivia walked home to ensure her safety while Olivia's father was watching from their house as she made her way across the lawn. Her father gave a wave to Sarah's father indicating she was home safe.

As Olivia's family was getting ready to go to bed her father knocked on her bedroom door, peeked in, and said, "Goodnight honey, don't be on the phone too long, ok?"

"Ok, daddy." Said, Olivia.

Then Oliva continued on her phone texting Sarah about the boys and all the fun they had.

It is Monday and both the girls were at school at their lockers when they saw the boys, the girls both started to laugh as the boys made their way over to them. The boys were a little mad at first and said, "Man, that was scary, we thought we were going to get caught. Why are you girls laughing?"

"Well…. it was… kind of funny!" they said.

"Then the boys started to laugh and said, "I guess it is now!"

After they chatted about what had happened over the weekend they went on with the rest of their day. A couple of hours later when school was out Sarah had to let Steve down gently telling him they can no longer be together.

Two years have gone by and Sarah and Olivia's birthdays are only a week apart; they both will be turning sixteen.

So a few days later their parents had thrown them a pool party and hired a D.J. to play music. They invited their family and some friends from school, even Olivia's boyfriend Jeffrey. About three weeks later they both learned to drive and got their license, occasionally their parents would let them borrow the cars to go to Fun-Land where all the teenagers hung out. It had a skating rink, bowling alleys, laser tag, rock climbing, an arcade, and a Snack Shack. The girls are old enough now to get jobs, Sarah started working at the local grocery store after school and sometimes on weekends. Olivia got a job at Fun-land in the snack shack which gets her discounts on all the attractions there. Sarah attempted to date again, but that relationship didn't work out either. Then she quit dating for a while, and tried again a few weeks later with another boy. She swears it was a curse for having red hair and freckles. Guess she had better things to think about.

It was soon Thanksgiving and Olivia's brother Mark was coming home for a holiday break. Carol was getting the house ready for the holiday. When Mark got home he gave his mom a big hug and kissed her on the cheek. Then, he sees Olivia, hugs her, and says, "WOW! Let me look at you, You're so pretty and so grown up already! Don't grow up too fast kiddo."

They laughed. He had a bundle of dirty laundry which mom washed then she got his room ready for him to stay in. Mom said to Mark, "After dinner I would like to take you over and introduce you to our neighbors I told you about."

So after dinner, they went over to the Johnson house to introduce Mark. Carol decided to take over a pumpkin pie. Olivia went along to see Sarah and hang out, but Sarah wasn't home. Helen informed Olivia that unfortunately, she had just missed her, that Sarah had gone out with a friend. As Carol introduced Mark to Mitch, Mark shook hands with Mr. Johnson as Mr. Johnson said," It's so nice to finally meet you Mark, how is college going?"

Mark said, "It's going well, thanks. I will be graduating in the spring."

As they got acquainted and talked a bit more. Mark tells him how he wants to become a producer then maybe even a director. After a long conversation with Mr. Johnson Mark said, "Well it was nice to have met you." Mr Johnson said "It was a pleasure meeting you also Mark and I wish you the best of luck. Take care, hope to see you soon."

When they got home Mark took Olivia out for some pizza to spend some time with her and she told Mark all about her best friend Sarah and how close they were.

He said," I know. I call mom occasionally and she fills me in on things around here." Later that evening Carol made a light dinner, they cleaned up, watched some television and they all went to bed.

It was Thanksgiving day. Mom was preparing dinner, Olivia was playing in her room and Mark and dad were watching football and chit chatting.

His dad asked, "So Mark, anything new in your life lately?" Mark said, "Yes, I was just going to tell you about this girl I met my second year in college. Her name is Stacy Reinholds, I would like to bring her home for Christmas and introduce her to you and mom." I was thinking after we graduate I am going to ask her to marry me." Dad said, "That's great son, can't wait to meet her, I will let your mother know."

Later that night in bed Harry told Carol all about Mark and his girlfriend Stacy, and his plans to bring her home for Christmas to meet them. Then when they graduate he wants to ask her to marry him.

Carol said, "That's fantastic news, can't wait to meet her!"

Then they turned off the lights and went to sleep.

It was black Friday. They ate breakfast then went out shopping. Mark went to the jewelry store looking for the perfect ring for Stacy, while his parents and Olivia were shopping. Later they sat down for lunch in the mall and Mark showed the ring to his parents. They said, "That's gorgeous Mark, she's going to love it."

Then they finished shopping and headed home. They got home and took all the gifts upstairs and put them away. They had a little bite to eat and later went to bed.

Saturday their parents had to go to work, as Mark went out to visit some old friends of his in the neighborhood Olivia stayed home and helped around the house and did some cleaning for her mother while she worked all day. Later their parents came home and Mark came in and Carol started dinner. After they were done eating and cleaned up Olivia got a text from her boyfriend. She asks her father if she could go out with Jeffrey for a while. Her father says "Yes but be back by eight o' clock." She said, "I will, thank you, daddy!"

Jeffrey picked her up, he forgot his wallet so he stopped at his house and they went in. Olivia wanted to go in and say hi to his parents anyway. They offered her something to drink but she said "No thank you." They left and went to Funland where they had fun skating, later they noticed the time so they left so he could have her home by eight o'clock. She went upstairs, took a shower, and talked on her phone. They all went to bed.

It was Sunday morning the parents and Olivia went to church with the Johnsons as Mark left to go back to college. Monday it was back to school for Olivia until Christmas break and back to work for the parents.

The weekend came and Harry started to decorate the house for Christmas just the way Olivia liked it, while Carol added Stacy to the Christmas list she and Olivia went back to the stores to finish up their holiday shopping. She didn't know Stacy yet but she will figure out something nice to get her.

Later after dinner they all went out and picked out a tree. They got it home and started to decorate it. Olivia helped mom wrap some presents then it started to snow. Sarah and Olivia went out to play, their fathers went out to help build a snowman with them as they had a snowball fight and made some snow angels. They went inside where Carol made them all hot chocolate as they warmed up then Sarah went home.

Well, it's Christmas eve day and Mark and Stacey came home with gifts for everyone. They greeted Stacy, with open arms as Mark introduced her and they took their coats. Mark took Stacy and their suitcases up to his room and showed Stacy where they would be staying. Carol asked, "Would anyone like some coffee to warm up?" Stacy offered to help get the coffee so she and Carol brought it into the living room as they sat around the fireplace getting acquainted with Stacy. Stacy tells them she is from Chicago where she grew up with her parents Darla and Arthur.

Later Carol made dinner, they ate, cleaned up and the Johnsons came over. Olivia and Sarah had a gift for each other. They exchanged their gifts with Piper also, while the grownups sat around and talked. Carol put out some snacks and offered some cocktails as they sat and conversed and laughed and the girls hung out together.

It was getting late, the Johnsons left and everyone turned in for the night.

Christmas morning Carol started their big dinner as Harry made breakfast for everyone. After breakfast they all exchanged gifts, Olivia was first to get hers then everyone else. Later they had dinner and everyone chipped in to clean up.

A week goes by and Mark and Stacy must go back to college to finish out and get ready to graduate. In the spring Mark's parents went to his graduation. When Mark and Stacy came home his parents threw him a huge graduation party meanwhile, out of the blue Mark tapped his glass with a knife and said, "Can I have everyone's attention please?"

Stacy just looked at Carol and shrugged her shoulders because she had no clue what was coming. He then asked Stacy to come up and join him.

He said to her, "You know how much I love you, and I'm so glad you came into my life. I would love it if you would spend the rest of your life with me?"

Then he got down on one knee. By now she figured out what was coming. She put her shaky hands over her mouth with tears in her eyes as he popped the question.

"Stacy, will you marry me!?"

She says, "YES, YES, I WILL MARRY YOU!"

They hugged and kissed as everyone clapped and congratulated them as they celebrated both their graduation and now their engagement. They stayed with his parents until they got their own apartment then got the jobs they wanted.

Six months later Mark landed a job in California after sending his resume to a production studio, so they moved out to the west coast. Mark was working at a studio, he is a producer for the film industry and Stacy is working in a chemist lab as a computer scientist. She studied biomedical engineering and science.

Well, Olivia and Sarah both graduated high school, their parents bought them each a new car, and off to college, they went! Piper was thirteen and wanted to follow in her sister Sarah's footsteps so she joined cheerleading, and played on the girls' softball team, she didn't like volleyball.

Sarah and Olivia both got into NYU but were assigned different dorms. They hung out as much as they could since classes kept them pretty busy with their studies. They got along well with their roommates. They joined a frat club, Sarah partied a lot and began to drift away from Olivia. She hung out with a whole different crowd than Olivia. Sarah lost a lot of weight and finally felt good about herself, she doesn't blame it on her red hair and freckles anymore.

They both graduated college and Piper was just going to college. Olivia got a job at Envoque. She took up fashion management, designing arts, and merchandising. She rented a studio apartment. Sarah studied Global business and got an entry-level job at IBM and travels a lot through her job. She hopes to move up the ladder one day.

Sarah would call Olivia on occasions like holidays and birthdays. They would get together and catch up on life.

Olivia and Sarah were invited to Mark and Stacy's wedding, Stacy had an older sister, her name was Tammy, she was going to be the maid of honor and Stacy asked Sarah and Olivia if they would be her bridesmaids. So Olivia found time to make all their dresses, Stacy and Tammy had to go to New York to get fitted and have their dresses altered.

Their families flew to California and stayed in a hotel, then Olivia gave them their dresses and they all fit perfectly! They met Stacy's family at the rehearsal dinner the day before the wedding. Darla and Arthur Reinholds and her sister Tammy. The wedding was beautiful. The next day they all went back home for work and Mark and Stacy went off on their honeymoon to Cancun.

A week later Olivia went on the computer to look up this guy Jack Creed whom she dated in college, so she typed in his name when a different name came up. A Jack Carter. She wanted to check out his profile and see why his name came up instead. Perhaps Jack changed his last name for some reason when he moved to Florida? He got a job there and they lost touch. Olivia had accidentally clicked the button on his messenger as he responded, "Hello?" She thought fast and asked, "Is this Jack Creed?"

He responded quickly with a "No sorry this is Jack Carter."

She was surprised and said to herself "Oh I'm not going to answer him; I don't know who he is." So she waited a few moments then said "AH what the hell why not?" She took a chance and asked again, "Is this Jack Creed?"

He said, "No sorry, my name is Jack Carter."

She said, "Oh I'm sorry I was looking up an old friend of mine, his name is Jack also so I decided to look him up while I was thinking about him, his last name also starts with a C."

They continued to talk. He was funny and made her laugh a lot. During their conversation, she brought up her friend Jack Creed again and said that they dated back in college but he moved to Florida and got a job. It's been a few years since we spoke.

"He told me to stay in touch but life happens," Olivia said.

Then she told him about her (sister-friend Sarah) and how they met. That they met in high school and graduated high school and college together, and how Sarah drifted apart in college.

"We have busy lives now with our jobs. Sarah's job keeps her busy traveling a lot so it makes it hard to stay in touch even though she only lives a few miles away." Olivia states.

Olivia then apologized for accidentally sending a message and disturbing him from whatever he was doing.

Jack said, "No problem, it is a pleasure talking to you, you can accidentally look me up anytime if you'd like."

They continued to chat for a while longer then he said, "I'm sorry if I'm keeping you up but I can't sleep."

Olivia replied, "That's okay, I can't sleep either, My head is spinning thinking about a new design for a fashion dress I need to make."

Jack said, "Oh you make your own clothes?"

Olivia said, "Yeah something like that!"

She didn't want to give him too much information about herself even though they continued to talk for two more hours.

Olivia said, "Well it's getting kind of late. I really should try to get some sleep for work in the morning."

Jack said, "I hope we can talk again sometime. I'd like to get to know you better."

She said, "I think I would like that."

They continued to talk on the computer for four months, then decided, maybe it is time to take it a step further and exchange numbers. So they did. They would call each other every chance they got for the next two months. Now they take it one step further and agreed to meet face-to-face in a remote place for the first time. They met at a Coffee House Cafe, Olivia waited for Jack at a table outside since she got there first. It was a warm sunny day in May. She was wearing a white spring dress with yellow daisies, a black belt, a white hat with a yellow ribbon around it, and white sandals. She was nervous but continued to wait. When she looked up, she saw a man walking towards her table. He was tall, built a little muscular, good-looking, wearing khaki slacks, brown loafers, and a yellow Polo shirt, he had light brown hair, green eyes, clean shaved, and a beautiful smile.

She stood up and said, "You must be Jack!?" He said, "I must be. And, you must be Olivia?"

She said, "I am."

She took her hat off and put it on the empty chair next to her, they hugged then ordered lattes.

Would you like to go for a walk!?" he said. "Yes," she replied, as she smiled. "I would love to."

He took her hand and she was surprised but liked it. They sat awhile on a bench as they talked and laughed. He said, "Look at the time, are you hungry!? You want to grab some lunch?"

She said, "Yes I'm starving." She is very slender, almost as tall as Jack, with blond hair, blue eyes, and a nice smile. After they ate lunch, he said, "Would you like to show me around town a little?"

She said, "I would love to, where shall we start?"

They started in Times Square for a little, then went to Central Park, where they rented a horse and carriage that took them through the park on a tour. After their tour, they got some dinner at the Coastal Grill and had some drinks.

Olivia asked Jack where he is from. He said, "I'm originally from Seattle, Washington but we moved to New Jersey after I graduated." She says "I'm from Seattle, Washington also!" As they sat and talked a while longer she noticed the time. "Oh look at the time, I should be getting home for work tomorrow."

Olivia's phone rings, she said, "Would you excuse me for a moment, Jack?" It's Sarah. "Hey Sarah, can I call you back later, I'm a little busy right now?"

She hangs up and says, "Sorry about that but, I just never know when she's going to call, I will call her back when I get home."

Jack said, "I must be going as well, I have some things I must do, can we get together again sometime?"

She said, "Yes, I would like that."

Jack turned to leave but stopped, turned toward Olivia, and asked "May I kiss you on the cheek."

Olivia replied, "Yes."

He holds her arms, leans in, and gives her a gentle kiss on her cheek. She almost melts. Then they said their goodbyes and parted ways.

She gets home, takes a shower puts on her nightshirt, and then, her phone rings, she answers, it's Jack. She answered, "Hello."

Jack replied, "I know we just left each other a little while ago but, I've been thinking about you and I just wanted to say good night."

Olivia said, with a smile. "Good night to you too Jack."

Well, it didn't stop there. What was goodnight turned into a longer conversation, then he told her how beautiful she looked and complimented the outfit she was wearing. Then he asked her if she made the dress she was wearing?

She said, "Yes I designed it, and put it together."

He told her, "It was perfect and looked very lovely on you."

She thought, good thing he can't see me blushing.

He said, "Let me know when you're free again, I will show you around New Jersey where I live."

She said, "Okay I would like that! I will let you know."

Jack said, "I'll be looking forward to it."

Then they said their official goodbyes and hung up. Olivia's phone rings again, It's Sarah, she thought, "Oh my God! I forgot to call Sarah back!"

She answered and Sarah said, "Why haven't you called me back!" (sarcastically). "I just got out of the shower and was about to call you! Why are you so upset about it!?" Sarah said, "I'm sorry, it's just I haven't seen or heard from you in a while, are you free for lunch tomorrow?"

Olivia says, "Yes I am, I can't wait to see you, I have some good news to tell you."

Sarah said, "Oh?"

Olivia said, "You don't sound too thrilled about hearing my good news, what's wrong Sarah?"

Sarah said, "Nothing, I will see you tomorrow then."

After work, Olivia met Sarah at the same coffee house cafe where she met Jack, they hugged and were so happy to see each other.

Olivia said to Sarah, "Wow, look at you! Love the new hairstyle, makeup, and weight loss, you look fantastic!"

Sarah said, "Thank you, well tell me your good news!"

Olivia said, "Why don't we order first?"

They ordered lunch then Olivia blurted out. "I met someone! His name is Jack Carter!" Then told her all about him and how they met. "Funny story huh?"

"Yeah, I guess." Sarah replied.

Olivia looked at Sarah confused trying to figure out what's going on with her. They finished their lunch and Sarah was getting bored hearing all about Jack.

Olivia noticed then said, "I'm sorry Sarah, here I am going on about my life, What's new about you?"

Sarah said, "Oh not much, you know me and my track record with men, I don't keep one too long and besides, my work keeps me pretty busy."

They both kind of snickered.

Olivia said, "I would like it if you would meet Jack sometime."

Sarah said, "Sure let me know when."

They hugged and parted ways.

The next day Jack calls Olivia and asks if she was free on Saturday?

She said, "Let me check my schedule." He said, "Hello?" Olivia says, "Yes I'm still here, and my schedule is clear. What do you have in mind?"

"I will pick you up at 10:00 a.m. and bring you to Jersey, show you around, maybe hit the beach a little and do some gambling in the casinos."

Olivia replies, "Sounds good, see you Saturday then."

Saturday morning Jack picks Olivia up. She had her bag ready with beach items in and Jack put it in the trunk of his car which is a Lexus. She was WOWED by it. He showed her a good time at the beach then, and in the casinos. They had dinner and made their way back to Olivia's place. She thanked him for a wonderful time. Then he got out, walked over to her side, opened her door, leaned her against the car, and had their first real kiss. It was very passionate, she stopped him before she got too excited. Then he drives away, she goes inside and feels like she is in heaven.

She called Sarah right away to talk to her and see how she was doing then the subject went right to Jack. Sarah said, "So what's he like?" "He's wonderful, Very good looking, well-mannered and dresses very nice too. I am starting to like him a lot but not letting my guard down just yet." Olivia says.

Sarah said, "It sounds like you're taking it one step at a time. That's good. Hey, Olivia, I just got back from a business trip. Can we talk some other time? I'm exhausted!"

They hung up and Olivia's phone rang again.

It is her mother, she said, "Your brother Mark and Stacy are coming this weekend and have some good news to tell us! Oh, I hope she is pregnant she mumbles. I hope you can come home and see them?" Olivia replied, "Yes I can't wait to see you all again."

Olivia was thinking "my goodness my phone is busy tonight, I better get some sleep."

Olivia's job is going well. She's designing clothes and helping the models get ready for the runway. She has been very busy all week; she hopes to have her own business one day with her own clothing line. Friday night she headed home to Washington to see her family. Stacy and Mark get to his parent's house first and his mother Carol opens the door. She saw Stacy's belly and said, "I knew it! Come in come in."

Mark and his father take their suitcases up to his room. His dad looked at him, hugged him, and gave him a pat on the back, and said, "Congratulations son, I'm so proud of you and all your accomplishments! Now let's go down to our wives and celebrate!" "Your sister is flying in to see you both for the good news." Carol and Stacy were in the kitchen. Stacy got a bite to eat. Carol asked, "How far along are you?"

Stacy said, "Well let's see it's September, I'm four months, I'm due February 14th. We don't want to know the gender yet. We are going to have a gender reveal party. Hope you all can make it. It's in two weeks. Besides, my parents will be happy to see you guys again." Carol said, "Of course, we will be there. It will be nice to see them too dear."

21

Olivia came in and was so excited to see everyone she rubbed Stacy's belly and said "I'm going to be an Aunt!" Olivia tells them over lunch that she has met someone. Her parents said, "Oh that's wonderful honey." "What's his name?" Olivia replies, "His name is Jack Creed, he's tall and very good-looking. Mark says, "Uh oh sounds like someone's in love!" He laughs as Olivia says, "No, I do like him a lot but we only went out a few times." Her father said, "I want to meet this Jack sometime. Just be careful young lady."

They had a good weekend as everyone left to go back home Sunday. Olivia got home and called Sarah, but she didn't answer so she left a voicemail, telling Sarah that she went home to see Mark and that they had some good news. They are going to have a baby and would like us all to go to California for a gender reveal/baby shower in two weeks. If you can make it let me know, ok well call me back. One week goes by and Sarah calls Olivia and says, "I would love to go to California and see Mark and Stacy, what should I buy for them?" Olivia said, "Oh gosh I don't know, anything for a baby but, nothing pink or blue. I guess a neutral color. Hey Olivia, I would like to meet this Jack friend of yours too. Can you make it next Friday night?"

"Perhaps we can go shopping first then meet Jack for dinner?" "That sounds good. I will have to call Jack and find out if he is available and let you know."

Then Olivia says, "Sarah this means a lot to me. You can stay at my place so we can leave for California the next morning."

With a quick response, Olivia rushes and says "I will see you next Friday. Talk to you later, bye."

Olivia called Jack but got his voice mail. She leaves him a message to call her back.

A little while goes past and Jack called her back and said, "Sorry I missed your call, I was in a board meeting. What's on your mind?"

"Well, my friend Sarah would like to meet you. Are you free next Friday night?"

He said, "Hold on please, let me check my phone calendar. Ah Yes, I am free next Friday night, where shall I meet you, ladies?"

Olivia said, "At a place called the Capital Grill." He said, "Looking forward to it. Oh, what time." Olivia says, "Ah say, 7:00?"

Next Friday night came; they did some shopping then they got to the restaurant first. They got a table and had a few drinks. Jack walked in, looked around, and saw Olivia. She waved and the waiter showed him to their table.

He kissed Olivia then said, "You must be Sarah? I am so delighted to finally meet you, Olivia has told me so much about you, I feel like I know you already."

The waiter comes over and says, "Hi, my name is Joe, I'll be your waiter tonight. What would you all like to drink?"

Jack says, "Could you bring us a bottle of your best wine please?"

The ladies looked at each other and whispered. "OOOH!" Jack heard them, as he adjusted his chair, put his hand to his mouth and cleared his throat, and smiled. As the night went on they talked, laughed, and got acquainted.

After their table was cleared off they sat there a little while longer drinking and having a good time. Later Olivia knew it was time to go when Sarah started questioning Jack.

"So Jack Tell me, where are you from? Where do you work? What do you do for a living? Are you married?

Olivia said, "SARAH! That's enough, you're embarrassing me!"

Jack says "No, that's fine, It's just that subject never came up before."

Then responding to Sarah's questions,

Jack replied, "Well I am CEO of a national bank headquarters."

Sarah was a little tipsy from all the wine she drank.

She looked at Olivia and said, "Nice catch!" Sarcastically.

Olivia was so embarrassed she said, "We must be going now, Sarah!" She told Jack, "We have a plane to catch in the morning. We are going to California to see my brother and his wife for a baby shower/ gender reveal."

The waiter brought the check over and Jack took it and said, "This is on me."

They got up to leave, Jack stood up as he adjusted his shirt and said, "It's been a pleasure to meet you, Sarah. Olivia nice to see you again as well "Hope we can do this again sometime."

As they left Sarah stumbled and Olivia caught her, then she looked back to see if Jack had seen it. Thank goodness he didn't, she thought. They grabbed a taxi to Olivia's place, she helped Sarah in and put her down on the couch, took off her shoes, and went to bed. Then she thought I better call Jack.

Jack answered and said, "Oh you miss me already?"

She laughed and said, "Maybe, first I would like to apologize for Sarah's behavior, and second to thank you for dinner for the both of us."

He said, "No problem, it was my pleasure."

"Well thanks again, I LOVE YOU!"

She thought "Wait, What!? I said it?"

He said, "Olivia! I LOVE YOU TOO!"

Wow! Olivia thought Now they both know how the other feels.

Come morning, Sarah had a hangover. Olivia said, "I made some coffee and there is some aspirin in the bathroom." But Sarah said, "I'm fine."

They grabbed their bags and all the gifts, grabbed a taxi, and headed to the airport. They arrived on time to board the plane. They arrived in California where they were greeted at the airport by Mark. The girls greeted him with a hug as they went to his car. He put their things in the trunk and headed to his place. Once there Stacy came to the door to greet them. Olivia gave her a big hug then backed away and said, "Oh my God! I'm sorry, did I hurt the baby?"

She laughed and said, "No silly you're fine."

Olivia took off her coat and blurted out, "So, when are you due? What is it? Do you have any names picked out yet!?"

Her mother Carol said, "Slow down Olivia, one question at a time." And chuckled.

They don't know what it is yet, that's why we are here.

Stacy says, "I'm due on February 14th." Olivia says, (with excitement) "That's Valentine's Day!" Stacy says, "Yes I know, we won't know the gender until we open that great big box over there! As far as the name we are pretty sure but, don't want to say it just yet. We have one for a boy and one for a girl."

The girls finally turned around and said hello to everyone, "It's nice to see you all again."

Mark and Carol put out a spread and everyone ate, then when they were done Mark said, "Drum roll please?"

They made the sound then, counted backwards from 10, 9, 8 when they got to one they pulled the string and out floated tons of pink balloons! "IT'S A GIRL!"

Mark and Stacy hugged and kissed. They were full of joy! They both looked at each one's mom and said, Mom. Carol... We are naming her, Emily Caroline Darla Hudskin.

Both moms said, "You're naming her after us?"

They were ECSTATIC! And hugged them both. They all had cake and then opened all their gifts and thanked everyone.

Later Carol said, "We should be going, I'm sure Stacy is tired, it's been a long day."

They hugged them and congratulated them both again. Then said, "It was very nice to see you all again, hope we can get together soon."

Darla said, "Oh don't you worry, I would hope we will all be there when Emily is born."

Mark took his parents and the girls back to their hotel. Stacy's parents are staying with them to help Stacy and Mark out for a while. Mark's parents and the girls have a plane to catch in the morning.

The next morning Mark drove to the hotel, picked them all up, and took them to the airport so they wouldn't have to take a taxi. They were waiting to board their planes. They all hugged and said their goodbyes. Their parents got on their plane back to Washington while Sarah and Olivia had to wait an hour for their flight back to New York. As soon as Olivia got home she rested up for a while then took a shower. She was missing Jack, so she called him.

Jack answers, "Hello, Olivia you're back from California!?"
She said, "Yes I got in about an hour ago."
Jack asked, "Would you like some company?"
Olivia answered, "I Would love some company."
He said, "I'll be right over."

They hung up. An hour and a half later Jack shows up at her door with a bottle of wine and some roses. She answered as she leaned on the door, and she smiled and he stood there looking so hot, all dressed up and smelling of good cologne, she invited him in. They closed the door and he backed her up to the wall and kissed her passionately. She stopped him before they got too excited. They went into the kitchen, she handed him two glasses, he poured the wine as she put the roses in a vase. They went into the living room, sat on the couch, and had a few glasses of wine. They talked and laughed. He then kissed her passionately again as they kissed all the way into the bedroom where he proceeded to slip off her nightshirt and she slowly unbuttoned his shirt. He proceeded to slowly slip her panties down as she lay on the bed. He slowly kissed her all over her body and made her feel like she has never felt before. Then he undressed himself the rest of the way and made the sweetest and most passionate love to her she could have ever imagined!

They continued until early morning until they both fell asleep. When he woke up he gathered his belongings, got dressed, and left quietly not to wake her.

A few hours later she rolled over and felt around for him but he wasn't there. She opened her eyes, only to find a note and a rose. Then, noticing what time it was she quickly got up, showered, and got ready for work and hurried out the door taking the note with her thinking, when she gets a chance later at work she will read it. When at work she had been so busy designing seasonal attire for the models to wear at the fashion show next month. She had to go to the basement for more material. She thought she would get to have lunch and read it, but she continued to work three more hours. All she could concentrate on was missing Jack and thinking about the note and what it contained. Later Jack called her to see if she wanted to go out to dinner. She said she will have to let him know later what time she will be able to get out of work. He said, "Call me when you get done and I will come to pick you up."

She finally got a chance to sit and have a little something to snack on and relax for a moment. She takes out the note and reads it. She was flabbergasted by the words he had written.

"My dear sweet Olivia, I've never met any woman as pure as you, you take my breath away. I can't wait to be with you again! Love Jack."

All she could think about was the love they made last night. She thought I'm going to call Jack. I am starving and need to see him. I can come in extra early tomorrow morning and finish the rest. So she called Jack to come to pick her up. He was in the area anyway so it didn't take him long to get her. They go to the same restaurant where he met Sarah and the waiter remembered them and asked if they wanted the same table. He took them to their table and asked if he could get them something to drink?"

Jack said, "A bottle of wine please."

Then Jack asked Olivia "How's Sarah doing since the last time I saw her?"

First Olivia thought, why would he ask about Sarah?

"She's good I guess I haven't heard from her since then, I don't know what got into her, she isn't herself these days."

"I don't recognize her lately, that's not the Sarah I knew."

They sat and talked then ordered dinner. During dinner, Olivia asked Jack "What are you doing for Thanksgiving?"

He said, "I go to my parents for the holidays, why do you ask?"

She said, "I was wondering if you could go to Washington with me for Thanksgiving and meet my parents?"

He said, "I will have to check with my mom, but I'm sure I can work something out. I will call her tomorrow and ask her, then let you know."

She said, "ok I will wait to hear from you then."

They finished their dinner and some drinks and waved the waiter over. Joe said, "Is there anything else I can get you, sir?"

"No just the check please?"

Jack takes the check, pays the waiter, and tips him generously as they leave. He took her home. She invited him in and they made love and he left.

The next day Olivia gets to work very early and gets started where she left off. She worked for days and had been putting in long hours and didn't get to see Jack that often but he called her every chance he got. He called one day and left a message on her voicemail saying, "I worked it out with my mom and she said, it is fine if I skip out on Thanksgiving dinner this year.

Then I told her all about you and my plans to go meet your family and get to know them. She is looking forward to meeting you. I will have to make it up to her." He says,

"Besides we have a big enough family anyway and I always like to sit with the kids at their table for dessert so I probably won't even be missed. OH, well I will wait to hear from you."

She called him back on the weekend and left a voice message saying "I'm So glad to hear you can go home with me to spend Thanksgiving and meet my family. I told them all about you and they can't wait to meet you too. I will call my mother and tell her to set an extra place at the table."

Then she called Sarah and asked, "Are you going home for Thanksgiving?"

Sarah said, "I was thinking about it, Why?"

"Can you be at my place that Wednesday? Jack is going to pick us up and drive us all to the airport." Olvia said.

Sarah said, "Jack is going?!"

"Yes, why do you have to say it like that? Sarah, do you have a problem with Jack being around!? I asked him to go since we are getting serious, I thought it is time he should meet my parents and get acquainted with them."

Sarah says, (sarcastically) "No, I don't have a problem with him being around!"

"Well, you're always sarcastic when I mention him."

"Well, I guess I will see you Wednesday?" They hung up.

Olivia was all caught up at work with all the different outfits and dresses for the models for the fashion show next month. She was proud of herself and her boss was delighted to see how perfect everything looked.

Well, it is the Wednesday before Thanksgiving and Sarah shows up at Olivia's with her luggage and Olivia asks, "Are you moving back home with all this luggage?"

Sarah said, "No I'm just taking some time off and staying until New years!"

Jack picked them up and drove them to the airport. They catch their plane and head to Washington. Once they got there Jack rented a car and headed to Olivia's house. When they pulled up to the house he got Sarah's bags out and offered to take them over to her house but she just said, "No Later!"

Then Jack and Olivia got up to her house. Jack had a bottle of wine, a box of cigars, and a bouquet of fall-colored flowers. The parents greeted them at the door and gave Olivia a big hug as Harry shook Jack's hand and said, "You must be Jack, Come in."

Jack handed Harry the bottle of wine and box of cigars and said, "I hope I bought the right ones, sir?" Harry said, "They are just fine Jack." "Thank you."

He then handed Carol the flowers, and said, "These are for you Mrs. Hudskin!"

"They are beautiful Jack. Thank you."

She goes into the kitchen and puts the flowers in a vase of water.

Jack said, "I'm going to go out to the car and bring in our luggage."

Harry said, "Jack, wait it's freezing out there I will go and help you."

They went out to the car and Jack told Harry, "Sarah came with us, she got out of the car, I got her bags and offered to carry them over to her house for her but she wouldn't hear of it and just said "No later!" and walked away."

Harry said, "That doesn't sound like Sarah, maybe she's tired."

They went back inside and took Olivia's bags to her room and Jack's bags to Mark's room. They are not married so they will have to sleep in separate rooms. They freshened up and Carol made dinner. They sat down to eat and have a conversation. After dinner, they cleaned up then they all sat around getting acquainted.

Jack looked around and said, "You have a beautiful home."

Carol said, "Thank you Jack."

Later they all went to bed. Thanksgiving morning Olivia came down, kissed her mom on the cheek, and said, "Good morning mom. Happy Thanksgiving."

She got a cup of coffee and asked her mom, "Where's Jack, he's not in his room?"

She said, "He went out dear."

Just then Jack came in all sweaty and gently rubbed Olivia's hand, took her cup, took a sip of her coffee, stared in her eyes and kissed her cheek, and said, "I'm going to hit the shower."

Olivia blushes. Mom smiles. Carol prepares Thanksgiving dinner. Olivia goes for a shower while Jack and her father talk and get acquainted. Later they sat down to a big feast, Carol had the table all set with her flowers in the middle.

Jack said, "Mrs. Hudskin, this all looks so lovely!"

She says "You don't have to call me Mrs. Hudskin, Carol will do."

At dinner, Olivia told them about the loan she applied for and that she was approved. She says she purchased a store and is going to make designer clothes and sell them.

Jack said, "Olivia you didn't tell me!?"

They toasted to her success. After dinner, Olivia helps mom clean up and helps with the dishes.

Jack comes in and offers to help but they say, "No thank you, you can take out the trash if you don't mind, It goes out in the garage in the can."

He takes the trash out to the can in the garage and sees Harry's old ford truck. He comes in and says to Harry, "That is a nice truck you have out there."

"Harry says come on let's go out, I will show her to you."

They go out and tinker with it a little then come in, grab their coats and say, "We'll be back."

They take the truck out for a ride. They are gone in about a half-hour, they come in and go down to the family room and watch some football.

Jack says "Sir, I would like to ask for your blessing in asking your daughter to marry me."

Harry says "Son, it looks like you make her very happy. She loves you, I can see it in her eyes when she looks at you, so be good to her and treat her right."

"Is that a yes? Sir!?"

Harry says, you don't have to call me sir. Harry is fine. Now I'm going to have to talk it over with her momma first but, I'm sure it will be fine"

Jack shakes Harry's hand and says, "Thank you, sir."

They light up cigars and have some wine. Jack says, "I don't want her to know, I want to ask her on Christmas day and would like to invite your whole family to my parent's house for Christmas. I think it is important that you all be there with her. If that's ok with you sir, uh Harry."

Olivia comes down and sees them getting along then asks, "What's the occasion?"

Her father says, "Uh... your brother's baby, Right Jack?"

Jack says, "Uh yeah... right baby."

Well, Olivia thought. "What is going on around here? Is it me or is everyone acting crazy?"

She goes upstairs and says to her mom, "Jack and daddy are acting strange."

Her mother says, "That's just men, honey, get used to it."

Olivia says to her mom, "I'm going to go next door to see how Sarah is doing and say hi to the Johnsons."

Carol said, "What do you mean to see how Sarah's doing!? Is she ok?!"

"Well, Sarah hasn't been herself lately, she seems to drink a lot then gets rude."

Olivia goes to the Johnson's, they catch up on life and Sarah seems to be ok. Olivia didn't say anything to Sarah's parents about her behavior. She goes home, Olivia and her mom talk in the kitchen as she tells her all about Sarah's behavior lately. Later Jack takes Olivia out for a drink to celebrate and have some alone time. Meanwhile, Jack was hoping Harry would let Carol know about Jack asking for their blessings to marry their daughter. Harry did talk to Carol about what Jack had asked, and Carol asked Harry, "What did you say?"

Harry said, "I told him to be good to her and that she looks very happy and I would have to talk it over with you and let him know later. I also told him "I'm sure it will be fine with you, what do you say?" Carol had tears and said, "Our little girl is getting married, guess she isn't so little anymore."

Harry says, "So, I can let him know we are both on board with this?"

Carol says, "Yes!"

Harry says, "Oh and she doesn't know anything about this, or that he invited our family to have Christmas at his parent's house in New Jersey to be there for when he asks her to marry him."

"That's when he's going to propose to her. So we can meet our new in-laws."

Carol says, "You mean I get out of cooking Christmas dinner this year? So I guess we will not be here for Christmas this year! I better tell Mark and Stacy the good news."

Jack and Olivia come back and Olivia sees tears in her mother's eyes and asks, "Mom what's wrong?" "Oh nothing dear I was just thinking about when you kids were little and how much you both have grown so fast, and that one day you will have a family of your own just like your brother."

She gave her mom and dad a group hug and said, "I will always be your little girl."

The next day Black Friday. Jack goes for his morning run, comes back showers, then he and Olivia go out shopping and have lunch. While they are out Sarah comes over to visit with the Hudskins she comes in and says, "Hello Mr. and Mrs. Hudskin, how have you guys been doing?"

Carol says, "We have been doing fine, how about yourself? It is so nice to see you again, you are looking good, did you lose weight dear?" As she kisses her cheek, then offers her some eggnog. "Would you like it with or without alcohol?" Sarah responded "definitely with alcohol please, and yes I lost a few pounds."

As they drank their eggnog Carol asked Sarah, "So Sarah how's life been treating you? How's your job going?"

Sarah says, "Just fine thank you."

Then Sarah asked, "Where is Olivia? Is she here? I don't see her."

Carol says, "No dear she and Jack went out shopping, they have been gone all day. I'm sure they will be back soon." Oh, I have to tell you, we are all invited to Jack's parent's house this year for Christmas, he is going to propose to her! Didn't Jack tell you?"

Sarah said, "No he didn't mention it. Well dear perhaps he will. Now don't you say anything to her, she doesn't know."

As Sarah mumbles under her breath (I didn't see that coming) Carol says, "What was that dear?"

Just like that she says, "I must be going now, thank you for the drink Mrs. Hudskin."

And she rushes out! Now Carol thought, "Olivia is right about Sarah, I wonder what's going on with her?" These girls were as close as sisters. I would think she would be happy for Olivia. Olivia and Jack came home and took their bags right upstairs. Olivia came down first and mom pulled her to the side and was looking out for Jack. Olivia, looking confused, looks around to see what her mother is looking for. She asked "what's going on?"

Carol whispers, "You are right about Sarah, she came over to say hi and I offered her some eggnog and asked if she would rather have it with alcohol or without."

She said "Oh definitely with please!"

And she asked where you were and when I mentioned you and Jack went out shopping, just like that she had to go. She thanked me for the drink and rushed out the door!

"Do they know each other? Did they date at one time or something?"

Olivia says, "As far as I know they are strangers, I introduced them!"

Carol saw Jack coming and quickly turned and walked in the kitchen. Jack saw them talking and said in a whisper, "WOW! Looked like you ladies were in a deep conversation."

"What were you ladies talking about? Everything ok?"

Olivia says, "Yes it's all good, just talking about the holidays."

As she walks away. Harry walks in from work and Jack says, "I don't understand women."

Harry says, "We never will, don't even try."

Later they watched a Christmas show, Olivia made popcorn and settled in for the night. Saturday morning Carol made breakfast, they all ate, cleaned up, and went shopping. They were shopping all day, then Jack said, "I am going to treat you all to dinner, anywhere you want to go."

So you won't have to cook today after that big dinner yesterday. They went to a steakhouse, had dinner and some drinks, then took all their gifts home and just relaxed and watched some television then they all went to bed.

Jack and Olivia had to pack to catch a plane to go home for work Monday. In the morning they said their goodbyes, hugged and were on their way. When they got home Jack dropped Olivia off, she asked if he wanted to come in for a while. He does. First, she calls her mom to let her know they made it home safe. As she's on the phone, Jack kisses her neck and hugs her from behind and she giggles and holds on to his arm until she hangs up. Then he couldn't wait to make mad passionate love to her since he couldn't do anything at her parent's house that just wouldn't have been appropriate. They made love, then they both fell asleep. They were exhausted. He got up, kissed her good night, and went home.

Olivia was so busy with her job and moving into her store, Jack helped her move in and hired a moving company to move in the big stuff. Now she only works part-time for the company and runs her store in the afternoons and Saturdays.

Jack called Olivia to take her out to dinner. While they were eating, Jack suggests Olivia hire a salesperson to help at the store.

Olivia said, "That's a great idea! Thanks Jack!"

After dinner, Olivia said, I better get home, I have to put an ad in for a salesperson. The ad read: LOOKING TO HIRE AN AMBITIOUS PERSON WHO CAN MANAGE A CLOTHING STORE AND DO SALES. MUST BE FLEXIBLE AND WORK WEEKENDS AND SOME HOLIDAYS. CALL (555) 277-1212. The next day she places an ad. She interviews several women and a man. She liked this young girl, Sheila. She reminded Olivia of herself, young and very ambitious. She had a background check done on her by her father. He got back to her and said, "She is clean also, she is young, single, and has no children. I think she would be a good candidate for the job honey."

"Thanks, dad I love you!" She calls Sheila and tells her she has the job.

Sheila says, "Thank you so much. You won't be disappointed. When can I start?"

"How's tomorrow?" Olivia says.

"I will be there. What time?"

"Let's say eight o'clock to get everything ready to open at nine."

For the grand opening, they have a ribbon-cutting ceremony and since her family can't be there, Jack FaceTimes them in Washington and California so they don't miss it. There are customers outside watching and waiting to go in and shop.

After she cut the ribbon everyone went in where Sheila greeted them and offered the customers a small glass of champagne and some hors d' oeuvres as Olivia walked around introducing herself and welcomed everyone to her store. By the time the store was ready to close the sales rack was almost empty, they counted up the cash register. It was a good turnout. Jack came back to give Olivia a ride and they offered Sheila a ride home so she wouldn't have to take the bus. They got back to Olivia's place and Olivia called her parents to tell them she had a really good day at the store and that it went well. Jack stayed over. They got up that morning and they both went their separate ways, Jack went back home, later he called Olivia and asked if she would like to go to his parents for Christmas and meet them.

She said, "I will have to talk it over with my parents and get back to you."

So she calls her mom and asks if she would mind if she would go to Jack's parents for Christmas this year."

Her mom said, "Oh honey you know how your dad likes to decorate our home for you. But if that's what makes you happy then I'm happy for you." "So I will let your father, Mark, and Stacy know you won't be here this year. Well, you have fun, we will miss you! Love you!"

Well her father was standing right there and said, "You were so convincing I don't think she suspected a thing."

Olivia was at the store with Sheila and it was getting busy, so she thought maybe I should hire someone to help out Shiela. So she placed another ad. This ad read: WANTED: SOMEONE TO HELP WITH SALES IN A CLOTHING STORE TWO DAYS A WEEK SOME WEEKENDS AND HOLIDAYS (Hours flexible) CALL (555) 277-1212.

So a young lady applied. She is a single mother looking for extra work. Olivia hired her. Her name is Ginny, she introduced her to Sheila and told her, "Sheila will be in charge if you need any help with anything, just ask her and she will help you. And if she can't then she will have to call me and I will come help with whatever it is."

Olivia showed her around and what she wanted her to do. She showed her how she wanted the hangers to face, all inward properly. Where the sales rack is and to remember if anyone asks if there is a sale item in the back in different sizes or colors, just tell them NO. What is out here has to go for new inventories, they are sell-outs.

She says, "I will leave you two now if you run into any trouble with anything don't hesitate to call me." She leaves to go to her other job where she still helps out. She does some paperwork, answers the phone, takes orders for other stores and supplies.

It's almost Christmas. Olivia stopped in the store to let Sheila know she will be leaving in two days to go on vacation.

Sheila says, "Olivia don't forget you have the winter fashion show tomorrow you've been working so hard on."
Olivia says, "Oh gosh! Thank you Sheila I almost forgot!"

Well Olivia goes to work and makes sure all the outfits are hanging on the racks for each model. And everything is organized and in order so the models can come backstage, grab the outfit they need to change into quickly, and get back out on the runway. She wants the show to go without a glitch. She thought that everything looked good, so she headed home.

Sheila calls her and lets her know she has the money in the safe and it's all locked up. The register is empty and all accounted for.
Olivia says, "Thanks for filling me in, have a good night."

Today is the fashion show and all the models are getting their makeup and hair done, it's chaos back here! The first model goes out on stage and the crowd is wowed by the designed dress. Some guy comes backstage and asks, "Who designed that extraordinary dress!"
Olivia says, "I did."

He says, "Can I buy it?" She says, "It's one of a kind." Olivia looks at her boss and she nods her head as to ask how much.

Olivia says, "How much would you pay for it?" The guy says "Ten thousand dollars! But you can never make a duplicate."

They were both floored at the price and said "Can we talk it over and get back to you?"

She pulled Olivia aside and they discussed it. Her boss said we will make out on this deal and I know you need the money with that store you just opened up."

"You have to pay your employees. What do you say?"

"Oh let me first ask Jack." She waves Jack over and asks him "What do you think about this guy buying my dress I designed?"

He said, "How much is the offering?"

She says, "Ten thousand dollars! But there's a catch, I can't make another like it."

"Did it take a lot to make it?"

She said, "No, supplies and time would only add up to about $150.00."

He said, "Do the deal, it's a no brainer."

They met back up with the buyer and proceeded to do the deal.

After the show, the guy comes back, they package it up, he gives her the money and she gives her boss a couple hundred.

"Who will you give that dress to?"

He says, "No one, it will be added to my collection."

Jack says, "you know where he's going to put that?"

"No."

"In his art museum" Olivia said, "It is one of a kind."

Well fashion shows are over now, and people are almost all gone.

She said to Jack, "I must go home and pack now since we are leaving in the morning."

He drove them to her place, she packed and then they went to bed. The next morning, they get up. It's Christmas Eve day, they start to head out and she says, "Can we stop at my store to check on things and make sure Sheila's ok first?"

They stop, she runs in and Sheila is fine. "It's a slow start", she says. "Well, have Ginny clean up and straighten out the racks, and make it look neat in here. She can run the vacuum while no one is here and clean the bathroom up. If you don't get too many customers, close at twelve today, and close for Christmas Day."
"You two can have off and enjoy your Christmas." As she gives them both a Christmas bonus of $100.00 dollars. "Thank you Miss Hudskin, Merry Christmas!"

She leaves and they head to Jack's parent's house. Olivia doesn't understand why they are taking her family's gifts with them to his parent's house. She is getting nervous and the closer they get she thinks to herself, what if they don't like me? Did I bring enough clothes?

They pull up and go to the door and his parents greet them. He says mom and dad this is Olivia, Olivia this is my mom Gail and my father Jack Sr. "Come in, you kids look cold, would you like some coffee?" Olivia says, "I would love some, thank you. Can I help you?"

"No dear you just sit and make yourself comfortable, you are a guest."

Olivia looks at all the family photos on the wall and some on the piano. She says, "Your home is beautiful and very festive. Reminds me of home."

"Thank you, Olivia."

Gail comes out with the coffee and they sit and talk and get acquainted. Meanwhile Olivia's family are on their way to New Jersey. They get to their hotel where they will stay for a few days. Her parents go to their room and Mark and Stacy go to their room. Carol texts Jack and lets him know what hotel they are staying at. Jack texts back, "I know where that is, just let me know when you folks are ready and I will make an excuse to get away to come get you all."

They freshen up, and Carol lets Jack know they are ready.

Jack says to Olivia, "I hate to do this to you but I must run an errand.

Will you be alright here?"

Gail says, "She'll be fine. Do you want to help me put a platter together?" She says, "Yeah sure."

They go into the kitchen and get some food out and make a platter.

Olivia says, "This is a lot of food! Are you expecting company?"

Meanwhile her parents come in and go to the kitchen, Olivia turns around and is SURPRISED! And so excited to see them there.

She says, "Oh my God, what are you all doing here!"

Carol says, "Well Jack thought it would be good to come to have Christmas here with you!"

Olivia introduces her parents. "This is my mom Carol, my father Harry, my brother Mark and my sister-in-law Stacy. Oh yeah and my niece, Emily."

As she taps Stacy's belly. Mom, dad, Mark, Stacy this is Jack's parents, his mom Gail and his father Jack Sr. Oh my God, this is so great thank you, Jack. And thank you Mr. and Mrs. Carter for inviting my parents here for Christmas to be with me."

They all sat down and had some hors d'oeuvres and got acquainted. They had some wine and talked for hours.

"Well, it's getting late, we should be going so we can get some rest for tomorrow." So they thank the Carters for having them.

Then Gail says, "It's our pleasure, see you all tomorrow."

Jack Sr. says, "Thanks for coming, nice to have met your acquaintance."

Olivia and Jack take them back to their hotel and say, "See you all tomorrow, love you."

They get back to his parent's house and Olivia helps Gail clean up, then they all settle in for the night.

It's Christmas day! Gail and Jack Sr. were up early and made some pancakes and baked some cookies. Jack and Olivia slept in a little then, took showers and came down, had coffee and breakfast. When they are finished Olivia helps Gail clean up as Jack says, "I must run an errand. I will be back."

Meanwhile back at the hotel, her family decides to have breakfast at the restaurant next to the hotel. Stacy sees a red-headed girl at a table in the back and says, "That girl looks like Sarah!"

Mark says, "Don't be silly dear, Sarah didn't come, we didn't see her at the airport or on the plane. It's just someone that looks like her."

Then a man walks up to the girl and now Stacy says, "That man at her table looks like Jack with her!" Mark says it can't be, he is at home with my sister and going to ask her to marry him."

Stacy was trying to get a good look but their waiter came to their table to take their order, and was in the way of her view and by the time he moved they were gone.

Stacy said, "Where'd they go?"

Mark was thinking, "Is my wife right? Was that Sarah and Jack? He is in the area to come to pick us up."

When they are done eating they text Jack to let him know where they are and let him know they are ready, as he walks in the door. They are surprised to see him so soon. Harry thought Jack looked a little nervous. So Harry says, "Jack you ok?"

Jack says, "Yes sir, I'm fine."

They get their coats on and head to Jack's parents.

Gail started to prepare dinner as Jack and Olivia's family came in. They all offered to help Gail with the rest of the dinner. So all the women are in the kitchen cooking and the men are in the living room watching football and having some beers. Mark and Jack went into the kitchen for some more beers and Olivia said, "Wonder why Sarah didn't come?" Stacy looks at Mark and his mom and Olivia says, "What?"

"Nothing dear, she was supposed to come but she never came over to go to the airport."

Gail says, "That name sounds familiar. Where do I know that name from?

What's her last name?"

Carol says, "Johnson, she is Olivia's best friend. They kinda grew up together." Gail stated, "I've heard that name before."

Jack quickly says "Mom you're thinking of an actress you were talking about the other day."

When the doorbell rings.

Jack says, "I'll get it."

"Sarah", Jack whispers. "WHERE THE HELL HAVE YOU BEEN! YOU TEXTED ME AND SAID YOU WOULD BE HERE IN A HALF AN HOUR!"

She says, "I'm here aren't I?" (sarcastically) She walks in.

He introduces her to his dad and says you already know Stacy and Mark."

They say, "Hello Sarah, nice to see you again."

Jack takes her into the kitchen and says, "Look who else showed up!"

Olivia turns around and says "Oh my God! Sarah you're here!" She goes and hugs her. They talk until dinner is ready.

Then Jack's older sister Sylvia comes in, shakes off the cold, hangs up her coat, and is introduced to everyone. They all sat down to eat. All you hear is chatter from all the different conversations going on. After dinner, all the ladies cleaned up except Stacy. They are sipping wine and laughing. Carol and Mark told Stacy to go into the living room and rest her swollen feet. She asked Jack Sr. "Would it be ok if I could go lie down for a little while somewhere?"

Jack Sr. said, "Sure." He shows them where the spare bedroom is so Mark can make her comfortable."

The ladies were done cleaning up and went into the living room. Carol says, "Where's Stacy?"

Mark says, "she is upstairs lying down, she is getting tired."

Olivia said, "now I know where Jack gets his sense of humor from."

Gail had us laughing in the kitchen, "you guys are funny."

They were having dessert and coffee. Stacy woke up and remembered Jack is going to ask Olivia to marry him and she didn't want to miss this.

She goes down and takes Mark's cup and drinks his coffee and takes a bite of his pie.

Gail says, "There's more pie and coffee out there dear if you would like some."

Mark goes out to get her some. Gail says, "So Olivia, Jack, tell me, how did you kids meet? I never heard the story."

Sarah says, "Yeah Olivia tells us how you met?"

Carol just looked thinking she already knew the story. Why is she asking like that?

So Jack starts, then Olivia cuts him off, looks up at him, and says, "I was on the computer looking up an old friend from college, his name is also Jack, Jack Creed. So when I typed in his name our Jack came up. I thought maybe Jack had changed his last name for some reason when he moved to Florida. He said to stay in touch but life got away from us I guess. So I sent a message asking if this is Jack Creed. He was quick to answer and said, "No, this is Jack Carter."

I thought oh, I'm not going to answer him, I don't know him. I was going to delete him and move on. But I didn't, I thought "what the hell why not, so I answered him anyway."

"He struck up a conversation, he was funny and made me laugh. We ended up talking for about two hours, we talked for months on the computer. Then we exchanged numbers and finally met face to face. And well here we are. "WOW", says Gail, "That's fate!"

Just then, Jack gets up and stands by the beautifully decorated fireplace, and asks Olivia to join him.

She looks confused but goes up and stands beside him, he turns, takes her hands in his and he says, "Olivia you know, I fell in love with you almost instantly. When I walked up to that table and saw you in that beautiful dress with the yellow flowers I knew at that very moment I wanted to spend the rest of my life with you. You are all I think about night and day and want to be with you all the time, I hope you feel the same about me?" Olivia says, "You know I do."

At that moment, Sarah excused herself and went to the bathroom, everyone just looked at her as she left the room. "I'm so glad you didn't delete me that day because then," Sarah comes back in the room, he just gives her a dirty look then continues. "I wouldn't be here right now asking you to marry me." She just stood there looking at him frozen.

Then he said, "Olivia, WILL YOU MARRY ME?" She had tears coming down her face as she said, "YES JACK I WILL MARRY YOU!" He opens a box with the most exquisite diamond ring, puts it on her finger, they hug and kiss as everyone claps and celebrates their engagement.

Carol and Harry hugged their daughter and said, "Congratulations honey." Jack Sr. hugged his son and congratulated him, as did his mother. Then they all shook Jack's hand and said. "Welcome to the family."

Olivia says, "Oh, now I know why you all were here. You were all in on this."

Carol says, "Of course, Jack wanted to make sure we didn't miss this moment. Besides, we got to meet our new in-laws. On that note, Mr. and Mrs. Carter, we would like to thank you for your hospitality and for inviting us into your lovely home. It has been a pleasure getting to know you both. You all have to come to Seattle to visit us sometime."

It was getting very late so Jack took them all to their hotel, except Sarah. She asked if they would mind if she stayed a little while longer to hang out with Olivia.

They said, "That's fine, just not too late."

They sat there talking and drinking wine. An hour goes by and Sarah says, "I'd better be going, you look very tired, and I must call a taxi back to my hotel."

Olivia said, "Don't be silly. Jack can drive you back."

"Jack, can you drive Sarah back to her hotel?"

Jack dropped Sarah off as Olivia stayed and got ready for bed and packed to head home in the morning. She has a store and job to get back to. Jack comes back and is acting nervous and Olivia asks, "Is everything alright?"

He says, "Yes it's all good."

Then Jack tells Olivia, "Since we are engaged I looked into another branch at the bank and found a job in New York, I thought I would stay with you until we could find something bigger."

Olivia was so excited and said, "I think that's a wonderful idea, then I would have you around me all the time!"

They go to sleep. They get up early and say their goodbyes to their parents. Olivia thanks them again for everything and they leave.

He drops her off and they go their separate ways. She gets ready for work then stops at the store to see how Sheila is holding up.

Sheila says, "Welcome back Miss Hudskins, how was your trip?"

She says, "Oh it was the best Christmas EVER!"

Sheila says, "Oh that's good, did something exciting happen?"

She shows Sheila her ring and tells her, "I just got engaged."

Sheila asked if she could hug her.

Olivia says sure. They hugged as she congratulated her. Then she tells her, "Ginny has been keeping up with the store and keeping it neat and in order."

Olivia looked around and said, "It looks so nice in here. How are the sales?"

Sheila said, "I kept the books up to date, they are in the back on your desk. Oh by the way, how did the fashion show go?"

"It went well, better than I expected. This one dress I designed, the one that was a high/low lace in the back with three dimensional butterflies that fluttered as you moved, sold at a very good price!" Then she adds, "Can you believe some guy bought it?"

Sheila says, "Things are really looking up for you. I'm so happy for you."

Olivia saw Ginny and told her she was doing a great job and would like to give her a fifty cent raise for such a good job.

Ginny was so grateful and said, "Thank you Miss Hudskin this means so much to me and my kids!" Olivia went in the back and called Sheila back.

Sheila went back and said, "You need something Miss Hudskin?"

Olivia said to Sheila, "You have been doing a fantastic job, I was just looking over the books and I would like to give you a $1.50 raise."

Sheila was so delighted she said, "Oh my, I don't know how to thank you!"

Olivia said, "Just keep up the good work. I know I asked a lot from you to mind the store shortly after you started, and I went on vacation and left you to do all the work, so it's the least I can do for you." Sheila said, "Thank you miss Hudskin, I do appreciate it."

Olivia says, "Please just call me Olivia."

Sheila said, "Ok Olivia."

So Olivia got busy on a new design for a pants set. Her phone rings, it's Sarah and she tells her she wants to have dinner later that she has something to tell her.

Olivia says, lCan I invite Jack?"

Sarah says, "Of course." Olivia calls Jack and asks, "If you're not busy, could you pick me up? Sarah invited us to dinner, she has something to tell me." Jack picks Olivia up and they meet Sarah at their favorite restaurant.

They all meet, Joe the waiter said, "Your table is occupied at the moment, would you like to wait or would you like to be seated at another table?"

Jack said, "We can sit at another table, that's fine."

Joe shows them to another table and they are seated.

Joe says, "Can I get you a bottle of wine Jack?"

Sarah says quickly, "Yes please. This one's on me."

Olivia asks, "What's the occasion?"

She says, "I met someone, he should be here momentarily."

As Joe gets the wine a man comes in and says, "I am meeting a party of three here."

Joe says, "I just seated three people. Are you with Jack and Olivia?"

He says, "I believe so."

Joe takes him to the table with the bottle of wine, and Sarah gets up, greets him with a kiss, and says, "Olivia, Jack, this is my boyfriend Nevan. Nevan, this is my best friend Olivia and her fiancé Jack." Olivia says, "Hello, it's nice to meet you." Jack gets up, shakes his hand, and says, "Nice to meet your acquaintance."

They drank as they got acquainted. Jack is entertaining them with his humor and they are having a good time. They ordered food and Nevan says, "So Olivia, Sarah has told me so much about you and how you two met. You two are pretty close. I don't have any siblings or have too many close friends growing up."

Olivia says, "It's sad and unfortunate that you don't because it's wonderful having a close friend to grow up with and share things with, like your feelings, thoughts, and dreams."

Nevan says, "Yeah but the best part of being an only child is you get spoiled."

They all laughed.

Nevan is kinda short, has black hair, tattoos, and dressed in jeans, a nice shirt, and sneakers, he is clean shaved. Nothing like Jack.

Well, as long as Sarah's happy that's all that counts. They all had a good time. Sarah finally looks happy, I think. Well, they talk about going to Las Vegas for New Year's eve as they are having dinner. So they all agreed to make plans to go. They finished their dinner.

Sarah said, "This ones on me."

They say their goodbyes as they thanked Sarah for dinner and congratulated her and told Nevan, it was nice to meet him.

The next day they made their reservations and got their plane tickets for New Year's eve day. The day before New Year's eve they got on a plane and the four of them landed in Vegas. Olivia was so fascinated with all the glamour, she said, "This is so beautiful, can't believe I'm here!"

They arrived at their hotel rooms and they are beautiful, nothing like Olivia as ever seen before. Of course Jack got a suite. They all got together and did some gambling. Jack was playing on the craps table, and was winning, he had Olivia blow on the dice and he won ten thousand dollars!

He said, "Let's go to dinner, my treat."

They had dinner, Jack paid, then they saw a show. They were living it up!

On New year's eve there were fireworks as everyone was celebrating. At the stroke of midnight Jack kissed Olivia, and Nevan kissed Sarah.

Olivia said, "I will NEVER forget this year!"

The next day they got on the plane and headed back home and back to normal life and back to work until they all got together again at Jack's penthouse where he invited some of his friends over and introduced his fiancé to them, as they celebrated their engagement. They have a little party and play some cards and games. Nevan is a lot of fun. He seems to be having more fun than Sarah. Olivia observes Sarah's behavior with Nevan and she thinks it's a little strange. They all make plans to go skiing for Valentine's day in Vermont. Some of Jack's friends and their wives said they would go along as well. After the party everyone left and Olivia and Jack cleaned up. So they all made their reservations for Valentine's day.

It's the day before Valentine's day and Olivia gets a call from her mom. Carol says, "Stacy's in the hospital in labor. She's going to have the baby!

Maybe Emily will be Valentine's baby after all!"

"That's GREAT NEWS! Thanks, mom, keep me informed! We are going to Vermont skiing, so if I don't get to my phone, leave me a voicemail, I can't wait to hear, I'm so excited!"

Her mom said, "I will dear. Be careful and stay safe, I love you!"

They get to Vermont and go to the lodge where they are staying and get settled in.

Nevan says, "I never skied before!"

Olivia says, "Me neither so, I guess we are virgins." They both laughed.

Jack and Sarah get a little jealous because Olivia and Nevan get along so well. They go to the lobby and get their room key and their tickets then go to their rooms. They get their gear on and go skiing. Jack teaches Olivia how to hold the ski poles, then he shows her how to sway back and forth. Nevan was watching as well, while Sarah was already going down little slopes and having fun by herself. Then Jack had Olivia doing cross-country skiing. She was enjoying it. Nevan was too, as they were slowly sliding alongside each other. Jack just stood there leaning on his pole watching them and laughing as Sarah's not around.

Then Jack pulled Olivia to the side and said, "Let's go in and get some hot chocolate and sit by the fire?" At first, Olivia thought I was enjoying myself, wondering what's wrong with Jack? She is confused, but they go in and Nevan is out there by himself and Jack and Olivia felt kind of bad for him but then they saw him talking to a pretty girl and laughing as she was showing him how to ski.

Then they were sliding side by side. Olivia said, "Good for him."

Jack said, "Olivia, that's not nice."

She says, "Why not?"

Sarah brings him along and doesn't bother with him.

"That's supposed to be her boyfriend!"

"That's just like her, surprised she's not drunk yet! No wonder she could never keep a boyfriend long; look how she treats them!"

Well, Sarah saw Nevan with this girl then she saw Olivia and Jack watching them out the window and how they were laughing so she goes over to them and says, "Excuse me?"

The girl walked away with a "screw you" look on her face and they came in and wanted to play charades. Some of the wives of Jack's friends were sitting there while their husbands were skiing. They were having some drinks and started talking to Jack, then he asked if they wanted to play charades with them.

They said, "No but, thanks for asking."

Olivia looks at her phone; she has a voicemail. "It's mom! Stacy had the baby! Well it's a little after midnight so that makes her a Valentine's baby!"

Jack says, "Aww that's wonderful!"

Nevan asks, "Who's Stacy?"

Olivia says, "My sister-in-law, I'm an aunt!"

Nevan says, "Congratulations!"

Sarah breaks out a bottle of wine. Then Nevan asks, "Boy or girl?"

Olivia says, "A girl whose name is Emily."

They drank and played games then Sarah blurted out "I want Jack on my team! If that's ok with you Olivia?"

Olivia says, "That's fine I'll take Nevan." They play a couple of rounds then Jack says he's tired and they go to their room. When they got to their room he turned around and said to Olivia, "WHAT THE HELL WAS THAT?!

She says, "What?" "All that bullshit of switching partners?!"

Olivia says, "I don't know I just went along with it no harm."

She says, with a little smile, "Are you jealous?"

He said, "No, forget it."

They make love and go to sleep. Sunday they left and went back home. Back to work.

It's spring and it's Olivia's birthday. Jack tells Olivia he wants to take her to see something. They take a drive and get to this big beautiful house.

She said, "Who lives here?" A lady came out and introduced herself,

"Hello, Im Jackie Roth, but you can just call me Jackie, how do you do?"

She says, "Jack, come in."

Olivia says, "How does she know your name?"

Jack says, "Don't worry."

Olivia says, "It's empty!"

Jack says, "Yeah go look around. What do you think? Take your time, no rush."

She goes through the place, looks at the yard, and says, "It's beautiful! But why are we looking at it?"

"Do you like it?" Jackie stands there smiling as Olivia says, "Yes I love it!" "Well, then it's yours! Happy birthday!"

Olivia says "REALLY!?"

"We have to go do the paperwork, then we can move in."

"Oh my God, OH MY VERY OWN HOME! I have to call my mom and tell her! Jack, I love it. Thank you!"

A month later they were moved in. Her parents came to see it. They were so happy for them. Mom asks, "Did you pick a date for your wedding yet?"

She says, "We are going to talk about that tonight. Look there are in-law quarters for when you guys stay over you don't have to stay in a hotel anymore or if Jack's family comes they can stay too." Mom shows Olivia pictures of Emily and gives her one to hang on her auntie wall. "She is beautiful!"

"After we get settled in we are going to have a housewarming party and invite everyone."

Months later all their families came, even baby Emily who is four months old now, and the Johnsons, Sarah and Nevan, and Piper who is engaged now too, and all grown up. Her fiancé couldn't make it, he had to work. They tell the family they set a date, it is AUG 25TH!

They all said, "Finally!"

Mark and Stacy said, "We are so happy for you and hope to hear one day soon about you having a baby."

Olivia and Jack were playing with Emily and holding her. Stacy said, "it looks good on you." As they all laughed.

Jack said, "Yes, Olivia it does."

Sarah just looked and smiled at Emily as Nevan saw her face and went over to her and said, "What? Would you want one too!?"

She just walked away from him. They had music playing and lots of food as they all looked around the house and admired it.

They said, "Jack, this is so beautiful, Olivia is a lucky girl!", as they all toasted to them. Sarah looked a little jealous but only Nevan noticed. Everyone was having a wonderful time. The parents stayed around to help clean up a little. Jack's parents went home; they didn't have far to go but Olivia's parents stayed in the in-law quarters which were all set up already. Everyone left, then they went to bed. Sarah and Nevan have been coming over to play games, they have been getting close and hanging out a lot.

They plan another trip, and they all agree to go to the beach. So they rented a beach house, a few weeks later off they went to the beach, the four of them again. They stayed for four days because they couldn't take much time off from their jobs. They all had a wonderful time at the beach, they played volleyball in the sand with a group of people, went in the ocean, and enjoyed the warm breezy summer nights alone being romantic (at least Olivia and Jack did). The cool nights were spent by the bonfire. One night Olivia couldn't sleep, she didn't want to wake Jack so she quietly tiptoed around as she saw Nevan come out of the room and go to the bathroom. He didn't see her as she stayed back and thought that's not the room Sarah chose to sleep in, why is he coming out of a different room? As far as Sarah and Nevan, Olivia couldn't figure out what she was doing with him because she didn't sleep in the same room with him or act like his girlfriend. Nevan saw Olivia as she started to head down the stairs.

He whispered, "Olivia."

She stopped and whispered, "Yeah." He said, "Wait up."

They went out on the porch as he lit up a cigarette.

Olivia says, "Why are you not sharing a room with Sarah?"

He says, "I snore too loud!"

Olivia says, "I remembered at the one hotel I saw you knock on her door and she wouldn't let you in, you looked pissed!"

He said, "She gets like that sometimes."

They enjoyed the night breeze for a while then Olivia said, "Good night."

And she headed back to her room as Nevan finished his cigarette then headed back to his room. Olivia thought "Why is she using him?" Whenever we play a game Sarah wants Jack on her team. It seems whenever Olivia and Nevan are around each other they are the life of the party. It is so weird, Olivia and Nevan laugh a lot and have a good time, sometimes it's like no one else is in the room. Jack is getting very upset about this. Now she is thinking Sarah is using Nevan to try to get in between him and Olivia. After three days They all packed up and headed home again.

Two months go by and she hasn't heard from Sarah. Olivia thought, "Oh boy another boyfriend is gone, at least that one lasted the longest." Olivia quit her job and is at her store most of the time now to make a new inventory. She has designed a lot of different styles and women are fascinated. She is now making men's clothing, like dress shirts and slacks for businessmen and women. Since she and Jack live together now, the first one home from work starts dinner. They are sitting there eating dinner as Olivia starts to say to Jack, "I wonder what's up with Sarah?"

"I haven't heard from her in a while, she must have broken up with Nevan.

Well at least he lasted longer than the other ones." Just then her phone rings, she answers, it's Sara, she said, "Can we get together Friday night?"

Olivia whispers to Jack, "She wants to come over Friday night?"

Jack just looked and continued to eat. "Just her, or is Nevan coming?"

Olivia played that off. She wanted to see what Sarah would say, to find out if they were still together yet, or if she dumped him.

Sarah said, "Yes and Nevan!"

Later Sarah and Nevan came over and brought some pizza with them but Olivia and Jack said, "We just had dinner."

So Sarah and Nevan ate as they talked about the wedding. Since Sarah is her maid of honor. It is getting close, the parents are arranging most of it. Olivia is so excited and nervous at the same time. Then Sarah says, "Hey, one last trip before you guys are married and go off together on your honeymoon? You never said where you guys are going."

Jack says, "I am taking her on a cruise to the Bahamas." "WOW!", says Sarah, "So what do you say about one last adventure!"

Olivia says, "I don't know we have been taking a lot of trips and I haven't had time to enjoy my new house much."

Jack says, "it's up to Olivia whatever she wants to do."

She says, "Just this last one until after we are married. Where are we going?"

Sarah says, "We thought we would just drive until we find the perfect place! No mountains, no beaches, just a quiet place to chill for a few days."

Nevan says, "No destination in mind, just us and the road. I used to do it all the time alone on my bike, just me and the road. I would stop in little towns and stay a day or two then leave."

Olivia said, "Give me till tomorrow to think about it and let you know."

They played a card game and then left. Olivia and Jack locked up and went to bed. They laid there and talked about it.

Olivia said, "I guess one more road trip then after our wedding it's just you and me for a while to make a life of our own."

The next day Carol called Olivia to see how things are going and to let her know they have a hall for the wedding, also a DJ and the caterer.

"Do you guys want to have fish, chicken or beef?" Olivia says "I will have to ask Jack what he thinks everyone would like and get back to you. We will discuss it while we are driving."

Carol said, "Now where are you going?"

Olivia says "I don't know Sarah and her boyfriend Nevan want to take one last trip before we get married and leave for our honeymoon."

This is all Sarah and Nevans idea, they said, 'No beaches, no mountains, just a quiet place and roam the country. Something about Nevan used to do it on his motorcycle and stay in different little towns so now Sarah wants to do it.'

Olivia's mom says, "She has to drag you guys along? Why can't she and her boyfriend just go? When will you be back? Do you think this is a good idea? I mean Olivia, with Sarah the way she acts with Jack now?!"

Olivia says, "Oh, it will be all right. Don't worry Mom."

Her mom says, "I don't feel right about this. You just get this house and you set off to nowhere land! Look, Olivia, I didn't tell your father about this stupid idea, and I don't butt into your business, but if I can't reason with you, then at least be careful and stay safe.

Promise me you will call me and let me know where you are staying when you get to wherever the hell Sarah is taking you."

Her mom pauses for a moment and then continues. "And how well do you know this Nevan guy? You know Daddy can do a background check on him if you'd like."

Olivia replies, "No. We don't have time, we are leaving soon."

Her mom says, "OK, honey. Please be careful. I love you!"

Then the four of them set out to find a quiet place to rest and forget all about everything for a while.

They pack for a two-week trip as they take turns driving through the night. They decide to stop at a hotel to take a shower, eat and sleep. Jack says to Olivia, "I don't like this, not knowing where we are going, why don't we just rent a car and go off on our own and enjoy a trip alone."

Olivia knows it's the right thing to do but she has her friend back and doesn't want to disappoint her so she says, "Let's make the best of it I'm sure it will be fine, besides we are together and it is kind of exciting! Isn't it?"

Jack has a bad feeling about this too. But, he is going to do whatever makes Olivia happy. They go to sleep. Olivia can't sleep knowing Jack is upset about this so she quietly opens their hotel room door and stands there breathing in the nice warm breeze as Jack sleeps. Then she sees Nevan come out and smoke a cigarette. She moves back so he can't see her as she watches what happens next. When he's finished he knocks on the door next to him. Someone answers, IT'S Sarah! Olivia was SURPRISED! Why isn't he in the same room with her again if they are dating? Olivia stood back so they didn't see her. It looks like they are fighting and she shuts the door. Nevan looks pissed off cause she won't let him in. Maybe he wants to have sex and she doesn't. He goes back to his room. Olivia thinks maybe mom is right, something is up with Sarah, why is she lying about Nevan. The next morning Jack goes for his run, comes back, and takes a shower, they go to the restaurant to have breakfast. Olivia is quiet and Jack asks her, "Are you feeling alright?"

Olivia says, "Yes, I'm fine, I just couldn't sleep last night." Then she says, "Why don't we just stay here?" The townspeople are very friendly and the town is so pretty and clean. It has a lot of little shops and flea markets where we can shop!"

Sarah says "No, let's move on to the next one and see what that one has."

So after breakfast, they pack up, leave and continue on their way to the next town. Nevan was hanging all over Sarah like they were an item but Olivia knows different and they don't know she knows. Sarah was being nonchalant about it. She had to do it so it did not look suspicious. Olivia just looked at Sarah with a concerned look on her face as Sarah looked at her and just smiled and nudged Nevan away. Jack was watching Olivia's face and was concerned.

He asked Olivia, "Why do you look so concerned, did something happen I should know about?" Olivia shakes it off and says, "I'm just really tired and my stomach is upset, I guess I'm not used to sleeping in so many strange places."

Jack said, "if something is wrong you would tell me right? I will take care of it, ok?"

He kissed her, and Sarah said, "Are we ready for the next town?"

They drove all these back roads, where there were hardly any other cars passing them but, they drove for another thirty miles.

Sarah said, "Are we all ready for the next town?!" They came to this small town. It was creepy and Sarah said, "WOW look at this place! This is it!"

Jack and Olivia both came out and said, "WHAT'?! HERE REALLY!?"

Sarah said, "It's the perfect spot!" they all said, "For what?!"

She said, "Look if you are all scared we can leave, but it seems quiet."

Olivia said, "Yeah too quiet, does anybody even live around here? It looks like a ghost town!"

There was only one little hotel with about six rooms and a restaurant, bar, and store combination. And lots of small cemeteries. They go into the hotel and get two rooms. Or Sarah made it look like they got one room but Olivia knows different. They settled in then went to the restaurant to get some dinner, but when they walked in the townspeople were not too friendly with outsiders. They all turned around and just starred with blank looks on their faces.

The waitress came over and said, "Hello I'm Lorretta, what can I get you folks?" Then She said, "Oh don't mind these people, they aren't used to many visitors."

They said, "Where are we?" Lorreta replied, "You're in nowhere land, that's what we call it around here. It's Called Cemetery Hill. Where people come to die!"

She started to laugh, and then everyone turned around and laughed. Jack and Olivia did not find it funny at all. Sarah and Nevan did!

Then the waitress said, "Oh come on, that's our little joke around here, we don't get too many strangers passing through to tell it to!"

As she giggled. Olivia said, "I will have a big breakfast with all the trimmings and a glass of orange juice." Everyone looked at her, Jack said, You must be hungry!"

She said, "I am starving." Everyone else orders a lite breakfast. They got their food and Olivia ate all hers plus what Jack did not finish. They go to their rooms and get settled in. While Jack goes for his run, Olivia lays across the bed and falls asleep. She wakes up and Jack is getting out of the shower. She says "I didn't hear you come in. What time is it?"

Jack says, "Eleven o' clock." She says! "wow! I must've been more tired than I thought. I'm going to take a shower then let's explore this creepy little town." After her shower, they go outside and there is Nevan smoking a cigarette.

Olivia asks, "Where's Sarah?" Nevan says, "I don't know she said an hour ago she was going for a walk, I can't reach her on her cell, there's no signal."

Olivia said, "She probably went to explore to see what was in this town." Olivia says to Jack, "I'm hungry, let's get lunch." Jack says, "Again wow this trip gave you an appetite!" They tell Nevan to let Sarah know where they are. They go to the restaurant and Lorretta says "You hungry again honey." Olivia asks, "Where's your bathroom?" Lorretta says, "Follow me." They go back to the bathroom and she whispers to Olivia, "So hun how far are you?"

Olivia says, "Pretty far we have been driving for days."

Lorretta says, "No hun I mean how many months are you?"

Olivia says, "Oh I'm not pregnant.".as she giggles.

"I guess you haven't told your husband yet? Don't worry honey I won't tell!" Olivia quickly goes into the bathroom, washes her face, looks in the mirror, and sees she looks very drawn and tired. She wonders, "Could I be?"

She comes out and sees a payphone and calls her mother. She tells her where they are. Carol says, "Just where the hell is that? Where did she take you?"

"Are you ok dear I am so worried about you; I hope you come home soon. Your father has been asking where you are and your brother and Stacy too!"

"Mom", "Yes dear" "Ah never mind, it can wait"

"Are you feeling alright dear?"

"Yes, mom, just a little stomach bug from being in the car for a long time, I'm fine, don't worry."

"All right dear but, if you and Jack want to come home see if there's an airport close by and fly home. We are all so worried and miss you guys."

"We are taking care of your house. Wish you were here to enjoy it, you haven't been here too long, then you take off with a crazy woman."

Olivia giggles.

"Well keep in touch dear, we love you."

She goes back to the table and Jack says, "I was just going to come looking for you. You ok?"

She says, "Why does everyone keep asking me that?" She orders a salad and some chicken fingers and fries.

Lorretta says, "Anything else? How about you sir? Do you want anything?"

"Yeah you have any wine?" She says, "no, but we do have beer." He says, "I'll take a beer please." Olivia says, "Jack! I didn't know you drank beer!"

He says "I don't, but I'm going to start."

She finished her food. Jack had two beers and they paid and left. They see Nevan sitting outside smoking,

Olivia says, "Those things are going to kill you. You smoke a lot."

Jack says, "Wait, how do you know?"

I just saw him earlier with one so I assume he does." Here comes Sarah all sweaty. They all asked where she's been. She says "I took a hike. It is beautiful up there on the mountain, it's a long walk but you have to come to see this. When you get there It's worth it."

Olivia says, "I thought you said no mountains or beaches! I didn't know until I went walking."

Olivia says, "You all go, I will wait here, have fun and take some pictures for me." Jack says, "I'm not going if Liv doesn't go!"

Sarah says, "Oh is that what we are calling her now?" With a smirk. Jack kisses Liv goodbye and says, "Go rest, we will be back." They are gone for four hours; Olivia is getting worried it is almost dark. A few minutes later Nevan and Sarah come jogging back. They ask, "Where is Jack?"

Olivia says, "I was just about to ask you guys the same thing!"

Nevan says, "You mean he's not back yet?"

Olivia says, "NO, WHERE IS HE?"

Sarah and Nevan just look at each other and shrug their shoulders as if they never saw him.

Olivia says, "He went with you guys where did you leave him?"

They said, he stopped to tie his shoe and told us to go ahead and he'd catch up, he never did so we assumed he headed back down to you." "Well he isn't here! I suggest you both go back and look for him right now!!"

They said, "It's going to be too dark now to see anything up there. We will have to wait until morning then the first thing we will do is go up and look for him, and if we don't find him we will have to get the town sheriff involved!"

Olivia says, "We can't leave him up there until morning, it's getting cold he will freeze till morning!" (as she is very upset and crying). She goes back to the restaurant but it is closed and no one is around. She doesn't know what to do. She looks at Sarah and screams, "THIS IS ALL YOUR FAULT, I KNEW WE SHOULDN'T HAVE LISTENED TO YOU! My mom was right, something is fishy."

"She said not to trust you because of the way you were acting around Jack like you are jealous of us cause you can't hold on to your own men that's why you go through so many and can't keep them!"! She just stands there and takes it as Nevan says, "Hold on a minute!" "All Sarah wanted to do was show you guys a good time and make up for all the time you guys lost, so don't put all the blame on her'! You didn't have to come."

Olivia says, "Who are you to butt in anyway? I don't even know who you are, or why you're even here! You guys don't even stay in the same hotel room together! So what's the deal?" Sarah says to Nevan, "You don't have to stick up for me, I'm a big girl I CAN HANDLE MYSELF!" To Olivia she says, "Well first off it's none of your business if we don't sleep together or what our relationship is! And anyway, how do you know we don't share a room? You're spying on me now?!" As she storms off to her room. They all go to their rooms; Olivia is crying her eyes out saying "Jack come back where are you?" She cries herself to sleep.

After hours of sleeping, she hears a bump and wakes up. "Jack is that you?" She runs to the door and opens it. There stands a big guy and she gets scared and closes the door. The guy says, "It's the sheriff, miss. Can you open the door so I can talk to you?"?

She opens the door slowly and says, "What do you want?"

"I want to talk to you about your fiancé." She opens the door all the way and says, "Did you find him? Is he ok?"

"No ma'am we can't search until morning when it gets light out. Besides, there's a storm coming so we have to wait till morning. Here in Cemetary Hills it usually rains a lot and fog at night until mid-morning. I just need to take some information down."

Olivia asks, "How did you know he is missing?" "Your friends here drove a few miles to find me and explained a little about the situation." So he goes into her room as Nevan and Sarah stand there listening.

Olivia says, "All I know is they all went hiking and lost Jack, they thought he came back here." "I didn't go. I wasn't feeling good so I fell asleep for a while and when I woke up these two were jogging down the hill without Jack".

The sheriff says, "Ma'am we are going to find him, it will be ok."

Olivia gave him a description of him, what he looked like and what he was wearing. Then the sheriff left. Sarah went to hug Olivia but she walked away and slammed the door. The next morning Olivia got up and went to the restaurant, Lorretta came over and said, "I heard about your husband, you ok honey? Would you like to use the phone to call someone?"

Olivia said, "Yes, please." She called her mom and when she answered Olivia was crying.

Carol said, "Olivia honey are you alright? I knew something dreadful was going to happen!"

"Momma Jack is missing, they can't find him, they went hiking and they came back and Jack didn't." Carol says "Slow down honey I can't understand you."

She hears her mom talking to her father in the background and she tells him what Olivia said.

He said, "Let's go get her and bring her home."

"Momma." "Yes dear." "I'm pregnant" (As she is crying) Her mom says, "Oh dear, we are coming to get you." "Ok, try to hurry."

Lorretta takes her back to the table and gets her some water and the sheriff walks in and says, "Olivia?" She says, "Yes, did you find Jack?" He said, "No but I have my best men on it and a helicopter up looking for him, we just have to pray and think positive."

She says, "I bet they know what happened to him. She was so jealous of him."

He says, "Now we can't go blaming nobody until we know the story." Hours later she is in her room and falls asleep. She hears a knock and jumps up. It's her parents, Mark and Stacy. She hugs them all and is so upset and crying.

Carol says, "Let me look at you, you are pregnant!" Stacy says, "Congratulations!" "Didn't you know?" She says, "No, I thought I was just sick from a lot of driving." The waitress told me it was because I was always hungry and sick at the same time." Olivia, Mark, Stacy, and Carol go over to the restaurant as Harry is talking to the sheriff. Carol and the family thanked Lorretta for looking out for their daughter. Harry is still talking to the sheriff and they are doing a ground search. He tells Carol to take Olivia home, he is going to stay and help look for Jack. Olivia cries out, "No I want to stay, I'm not leaving without Jack!"

Jack's parents come to see if there is any news about their son and Carol greets them and tells them Olivia is pregnant. Gail hugs Olivia but doesn't know what to say. So her mom takes her into her room and tells Olivia to get some sleep. As she sleeps, Carol and Jack's parents step out to see what's going on and now the news reporters are there broadcasting the search for a missing person and the townspeople are all watching. Oliva sleeps for a little while and has a bad dream that Jack is badly hurt and she can't get to him because she is holding a baby. She hears all the commotion and quickly wakes up out of her dream and goes outside. Her mom hands her a cup of tea.

Olivia says, "Anything yet?"

"No. Olivia, let us take you home."

"We are not doing any good here, you need to see a doctor and get some good rest."

She says, "OK but the minute daddy hears something I want to know!"

They see one of the searchers come running towards the sheriff with something in their hand and hands it to the sheriff. He looks at Olivia and starts walking toward her as she runs to him and says, "What is it?"

He shows her a sneaker and asks if it looks familiar.

She says, "Yes it's Jacks. Where did you find it?"

Jack's parents go over and look and Gail starts crying. The sheriff says, "On a cliff."

Olivia turns to Gail and they hug as they both start crying.

The sheriff says, "Now this doesn't mean anything he could have lost it. We will keep looking for him." Jack's parents are going to stay, they are going to pay for Olivia's room and stay there. Olivia's family all say goodbye to Mr. and Mrs. Carter and tell them, "You know anything, anything at all please, don't hesitate to call us right away anytime."

Mrs. Carter said, "I will."

"Tell Olivia we love her and to take care of herself and the baby, and to get some rest!"

As the rest of them head home they get back, her mother makes her rest, then calls the doctor. As soon as Olivia gets up her mother takes her to see the doctor. He examines her and confirms she is two months pregnant. He prescribed some meds to help her sleep and get some rest during her ordeal. Later she goes to her store to try to work and keep herself busy.

Sheila and Ginny said They are so sorry for what she is going through.

They said, if she needs more time off they can take care of things.

Then Ginny tells her "I know how to run the sewing machine. If you want me to finish some garments you started I would be glad to help out."

Olivia said, "That would be a big help, thank you both." Then she told them she is pregnant as they congratulated her.

Sheila asked, "If she could give her a hug?"

She said, "That would be comforting. Thank you."

She had enough merchandise to stay afloat to stay in business. A few days go by and Harry has to take Sarah and Nevan in for questioning, since they were the last two to see Jack alive. Sarah and Nevan get interrogated in separate rooms. Sarah's father represents her in the interrogation room. They are not to leave town. Olivia says, she will never forgive Sarah. It is four months now and Sara and Nevan are not found guilty because they don't have enough evidence of any foul play and no body found. So they were let go. It's October and Stacy, Gail, and Carol gave Olivia a baby shower. They invited Sheila and Ginny. Jack's whole family including his sister Sylvia, aunts, and Grandma. Olivia gets a lot of gifts and thanks everyone for coming and being there for her. Then she says, as she cries, "I wish Jack could be here to celebrate with us."

Then she cries harder, her mom says, "What's wrong honey?"

"Jack didn't even know I was pregnant!"

"Oh honey I'm sure he knows, he's here in spirit."

Three months later, on January 18th Olivia had her baby. It's a boy! She names him Jack the 3rd. Jack's parents come to see the baby and take him for some weekends. Olivia's parents move in with her and they live in the in-law's quarters. They semi-retire to stay with her until she gets back on her feet again. And they are happy grandparents. Harry becomes a detective and is still working on the case. They had to give up the search now. Meanwhile, Carol helps out with the baby and at the store some days.

The End

Printed in the United States
by Baker & Taylor Publisher Services